Little Baby Buttercup

LINDA ASHMAN • ILLUSTRATED BY YOU BYUN

Nancy Paulsen Books ☙ An Imprint of Penguin Group (USA)

For "Bob" and the Larchmont Boulevard days—L.A.

To all of my grandparents—Y.B.

NANCY PAULSEN BOOKS
Published by the Penguin Group
Penguin Group (USA) LLC
375 Hudson Street
New York, NY 10014

USA | Canada | UK | Ireland | Australia
New Zealand | India | South Africa | China
penguin.com
A Penguin Random House Company

Library of Congress Cataloging-in-Publication Data
Ashman, Linda.
Little Baby Buttercup / Linda Ashman ; illustrated by You Byun.
pages cm
Summary: A mother and baby have fun spending the day together as they play, work in the garden, visit the park, and more.
[1. Stories in rhyme. 2. Babies—Fiction. 3. Mother and child—Fiction.] I. Byun, You, illustrator. II. Title.
PZ8.3.A775Lit 2015   [E]—dc23   2014009896

Manufactured in China by South China Printing Co. Ltd.
ISBN 978-0-399-16763-8
1 3 5 7 9 10 8 6 4 2

Design by Marikka Tamura. Text set in Sassoon Primary Com.
The art was created using paintbrushes and ink on watercolor paper,
and then manipulated digitally.

Littie Baby Buttercup,
how I love to scoop you up.

Scoop you up and hold you near.
Kiss your little baby ear.

Hungry tummy. Time to eat.

To the kitchen. In your seat.

Hand, mouth, cheek, hair—
some to eat, some to wear.

Busy builder,
stacking blocks.

Take another from the box.

Stack them higher—
eight . . .
nine . . .
ten!

Watch them topple.

Start again.

Little Baby Buttercup,
on my shoulders, so high up.

Peek through branches—what a view!

Hello, bluebird. How are you?

Garden helper with a hose.

Spray the daisy,
spray the rose.

Spray the bushes,
spray the tree.

Whoa there, baby—
don't spray me!

Happy traveler, on a stroll.
Up the hill, then down we roll.
One more turn—
our journey ends.

Hello, park!
Hello, friends!

Bouncy baby on a frog.

Climb a rope,
then cross a log.

Up the ladder, down the slide.

Check the tunnel.

Who's inside?

Little Baby Buttercup,
to the swings,

then up, up, up!

Spy a squirrel.

Pet a pooch.

Oh—a soggy doggy smooch!

Wobbly baby,
toddling fast.

Oops—a tumble on the grass.

First, a bandage. Then, a kiss.

And another,
just like this.

Plip, plop. Time to stop.

Duck into a coffee shop.

Find a table, share a treat.
Watch the people on the street.

Shiny slickers.

Soggy hat . . .

Then the rain ends—
just like that.

Little Baby Buttercup,

look how fast
you're growing up!

Every day brings something new—

lucky me,
to be with you.